Women scientists in chemistry

TRACEY KELLY

raintree

a Capstone company — publishers for children

Raintree is an imprint of Capstone Global Library Limited, a company incorporated in England and Wales having its registered office at 264 Banbury Road, Oxford, OX2 7DY – Registered company number: 6695582

www.raintree.co.uk
myorders@raintree.co.uk

© Brown Bear Books Ltd 2021
This edition published by Raintree in 2021

Created by Brown Bear Books Ltd
Text and Editor: Nancy Dickmann
Designer and Illustrator: Supriya Sahai
Editorial Director: Lindsey Lowe
Children's Publisher: Anne O'Daly
Design Manager: Keith Davis
Picture Manager: Sophie Mortimer
Printed and bound in India

ISBN 978 1 4747 9859 4 (hardback)
ISBN 978 1 4747 9865 5 (paperback)

British Library Cataloguing in Publication Data
A full catalogue record for this book is available from the British Library

Concept development: Square and Circus / Brown Bear Books Ltd

Picture Credits
Getty Images: Bettmann 32; istockphoto: Steve Debenport 5; Library of Congress: 10; National Library of Medicine: 38; Public Domain: 14, 17t, 27, 29t, 29b, 41t, 41b; Bodleian Treasures 34, MIT 9, Popular Science Monthly 15, Rosalind Franklin University of Medicine and Science 40; Royal Society of Chemistry 16, Smith College Archives 8, Smithsonian Archives 35, Department of History/Washington State Univesity 11; Robert Hunt Library: 26; Science Photo Library: Library of Congress 17b; Shutterstock: 28, Kevin H Knuth 33, Mark Lorch 39; Wellcome Images: 4, 20, 21, 22.

Character artwork © Supriya Sahai
All other artwork © Brown Bear Books Ltd

Every effort has been made to contact copyright holders of material reproduced in this book. Any omissions will be rectified in subsequent printings if notice is given to the publisher.

All the internet addresses (URLs) given in this book were valid at the time of going to press. However, due to the dynamic nature of the internet, some addresses may have changed, or sites may have changed or ceased to exist since publication. While the author and publisher regret any inconvenience this may cause readers, no responsibility for any such changes can be accepted by either the author or the publisher.

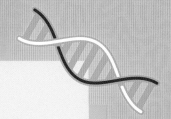

contents

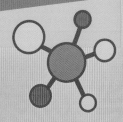

chemistry in time

From the early days of humankind, people have studied the way substances behave. The science of modern chemistry comes from the medieval practice of alchemy.

Alchemists working in Europe in the Middle Ages believed that matter could be transformed into another substance. They tried to turn common metals into gold. The experiments did not work. But although alchemy was based partly on magic, the idea of working with matter paved the way for the field of chemistry.

An alchemist studies ways to turn common elements into gold during the Middle Ages.

More women than ever before are choosing careers in chemistry.

Chemists study the substances and processes that make up everything in the world and life itself. They look at the way matter is made up of molecules and the tiniest particles. They study how substances react and combine with each other. Fields of chemistry focus on different things, such as medicine or the environment.

MAKING THEIR MARK

Traditionally, men have dominated chemistry. However, since the mid-1800s, women have made exciting advances. Marie Curie and her daughter worked with radioactive elements, and Rosalind Franklin helped to uncover the structure of DNA. But women often had to fight hard to follow their dream. Many were the first female students to attend universities. These trailblazing women became leaders in their scientific fields. They ignored prejudice to make the world a better place through hard work and creative thinking. These superwomen continue to inspire new generations of women scientists.

Ellen H. Swallow Richards

American chemist Ellen H. Swallow Richards pioneered the fields of water quality standards and home economics.

Ellen H. Swallow Richards was born on 3 December 1842 in Dunstable, Massachusetts. She was homeschooled by her parents, who were teachers. Ellen's family was poor, so she had to work as a tutor and clean houses to earn enough money to attend college. By 1868, she had saved enough money to attend Vassar College in Poughkeepsie, New York. After graduation, Ellen tried to get a job as a chemistry apprentice, but all her applications were turned down.

QUICK FACTS
....

NAME: Ellen H. Swallow Richards

BIRTH: 1842, Dunstable, Massachusetts, USA

EDUCATION: Vassar College, Massachusetts Institute of Technology (MIT)

OCCUPATION: Chemist

❝ You cannot make women contented with cooking and cleaning, and you need not try. ❞

BREAKING DOWN BARRIERS

Ellen was determined to take her studies in chemistry further. In 1871, she was admitted to the Massachusetts Institute of Technology (MIT). This was an all-male school at that time. Ellen became the first woman in the United States to be accepted at a scientific college. At MIT, she earned her second bachelor's degree and wrote a paper on her analysis of iron ore.

MIT would not let her study for a doctorate degree – they had not even granted a PhD to a man yet. But Ellen would not give up her work. In 1876, she established the Women's Laboratory at MIT, where she worked as an unpaid instructor. Ellen taught subjects such as chemical analysis, mineralogy and industrial chemistry.

In 1875, Ellen had married Robert Hallowell Richards. He was the head of MIT's mining engineering department.

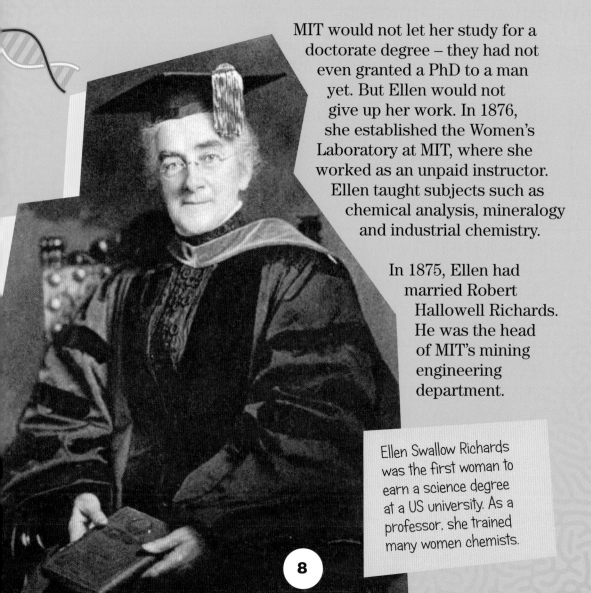

Ellen Swallow Richards was the first woman to earn a science degree at a US university. As a professor, she trained many women chemists.

MIT's first laboratory of sanitary chemistry was set up in 1883.

In the late 1800s, women usually stopped working when they got married. But when Ellen married Robert, he supported his new wife's career. He encouraged her to continue working and donated $1,000 a year to the Women's Laboratory.

SANITARY ENGINEERING

In 1883, MIT opened the first laboratory of sanitary chemistry in the United States. Ellen became assistant chemist. She researched sewage treatment and analysed around 40,000 samples. Praised for the accuracy of her work, she became an instructor for MIT's sanitary engineering programme in 1890.

Ellen and her team carried out a huge survey of the water quality of Massachusetts' inland waters. The waters were polluted with sewage and industrial waste from nearby cities.

> **The quality of life depends upon the ability of society to teach its members how to live in harmony with their environment.**

This groundbreaking work led to the nation's first modern sewage treatment plant, in Lowell, Massachusetts. It set a precedent for water quality standards throughout the United States. Ellen became a water analyst for the State Board of Health in 1887.

HOME ECONOMICS

Ellen was interested in applying scientific principles to everyday life. She wanted to teach people about the importance of being healthy, and "healthy" meant keeping a clean house with proper sanitation, serving nutritious food and being physically fit. To help people learn first-hand about food safety, Ellen set up model kitchens and opened them to the public.

Ellen's work set new standards for water quality. It led to cleaner water and sewage systems, like this one, built in 1896.

Ellen's work inspired the formal study of home economics. This is a food lab in Washington State in the early 1900s.

This area of study became known as home economics. It has been taught in schools ever since. Ellen held home economics summer conferences in Lake Placid, New York. In 1908, she became first president of the American Home Economics Association, which grew out of the conferences. She died in 1911.

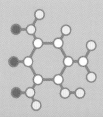

HEALTHY HOMES

In 1862, Ellen wrote the book *The Chemistry of Cooking and Cleaning: A Manual for Housekeepers*. Subjects included were nutrition for families, proper clothing, sanitation, physical exercise and time management for housewives. Ellen hoped that this information would shorten housework time, so that women could pursue other activities.

Ellen's book on housekeeping established home economics as a field of study.

Agnes Pockels

German chemist Agnes Pockels was a pioneer in surface science. She performed experiments in her kitchen while looking after her parents' house.

Agnes Pockels was born in Venice, Italy, on 14 February 1862. The family moved to Brunswick, Germany, when she was nine years old. Her father had caught malaria while he was in the army, and Agnes had to care for him and her mother throughout their lives. Agnes was always keenly interested in science, but the local girls' school she attended did not teach it. She yearned to study science at university but was denied that opportunity too – in the 1880s, young women in Europe were not allowed to go to university.

❝ I had a passionate interest in natural science, especially physics, and would have liked to study. ❞

KITCHEN SCIENCE

This did not stop Agnes from setting up her own laboratory, however. One day, while washing the dishes, she noticed that different substances floating on the water's surface behaved in different ways. Fascinated, she began to perform experiments to test how oils, dirt and soaps sat on the surface of water – in other words, how they affected the surface tension of water.

Agnes set up a simple device in her kitchen. It was later known as the "Pockels trough". She used it to perform her experiments. Meanwhile, her younger brother, Friedrich, was studying physics at the University of Göttingen, and in 1890 he sent Agnes an interesting paper. It was written by British physicist Lord Rayleigh (John William Strutt), who described conducting experiments similar to Agnes'. Friedrich urged Agnes to get in touch with Lord Rayleigh.

As a young women, Agnes Pockels cared for her sickly parents while also developing her scientific ideas.

Lord Rayleigh was a renowned physicist who experimented with light, sound and gases. In 1904, he won the Nobel Prize in Physics.

SURPRISING RESULTS

In January 1891, Agnes wrote to Rayleigh about her surface experiments and the results. Intrigued, Rayleigh asked his wife to translate the letter from German into English. What he read amazed him. Here was a young woman with no formal training or equipment, who had come to scientific conclusions that rivalled those of a trained chemist.

Although Agnes had told Rayleigh that he could use her findings for his own work, he gave her full credit for her research. He sent Agnes' letter to *Nature* magazine, and in March 1891, the journal published her words under her own name. Agnes' work became world-famous. She wrote many more articles before her work was interrupted by the death of Friedrich in 1913 and World War I (1914–1918).

❝ Regarding your question about my personal circumstances, I am really a lady. ❞

Agnes in a letter
to Lord Rayleigh

RECOGNITION AND AWARDS

Agnes' work established the principles for a branch of chemistry called surface science. Among other things, surface science is important in understanding and preventing the contamination of drinking water. American chemist Irving Langmuir became interested in Agnes' work. In 1917, he began using Agnes' research, adapting the Pockels trough for use in his own studies. He experimented with oil films on the surface of water and other liquids. In 1932, Langmuir won the Nobel Prize in Chemistry for his work.

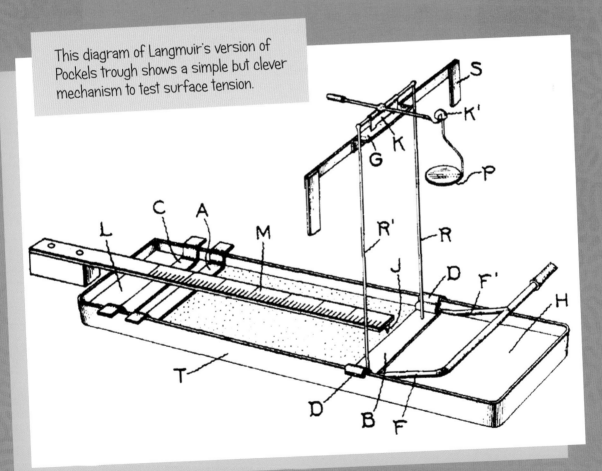

This diagram of Langmuir's version of Pockels trough shows a simple but clever mechanism to test surface tension.

In 1931, Agnes Pockels became the first women to win the Laura R. Leonard Prize from the German Colloid Society. Then, to celebrate her 70th birthday in 1932, she was given an honorary doctorate from the Technical University of Brunswick, in Germany. Agnes Pockels died in 1935, having lived long enough to see her extraordinary work recognized worldwide.

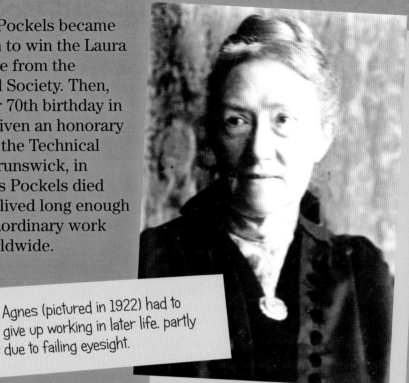

Agnes (pictured in 1922) had to give up working in later life. partly due to failing eyesight.

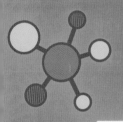

INSPIRED BY AGNES

American chemist Irving Langmuir studied Pockels' work and used it to make other important discoveries in surface science. Langmuir, along with many other chemists, acknowledged his debt to Agnes and her astonishing contributions to the field of chemistry. Langmuir went on to receive many prestigious awards in the fields of chemistry and physics.

Irving Langmuir (left) with inventor Guglielmo Marconi in the General Electric Research Lab where he worked in New York. 1922.

marie curie and irène Joliot-curie

Chemists Marie Curie and her daughter Irène Joliot-Curie made history with their research into radioactivity and the discovery of new elements.

Nuclear chemist Marie Sklodowska Curie is perhaps the most famous woman scientist in history. She was born into a well-educated family in Warsaw, Poland, on 7 November 1867. The young Marie loved science. After finishing school, she wanted to go on and study the subject at university. However, Marie was turned down by the universities in Poland and Austria because she was a woman.

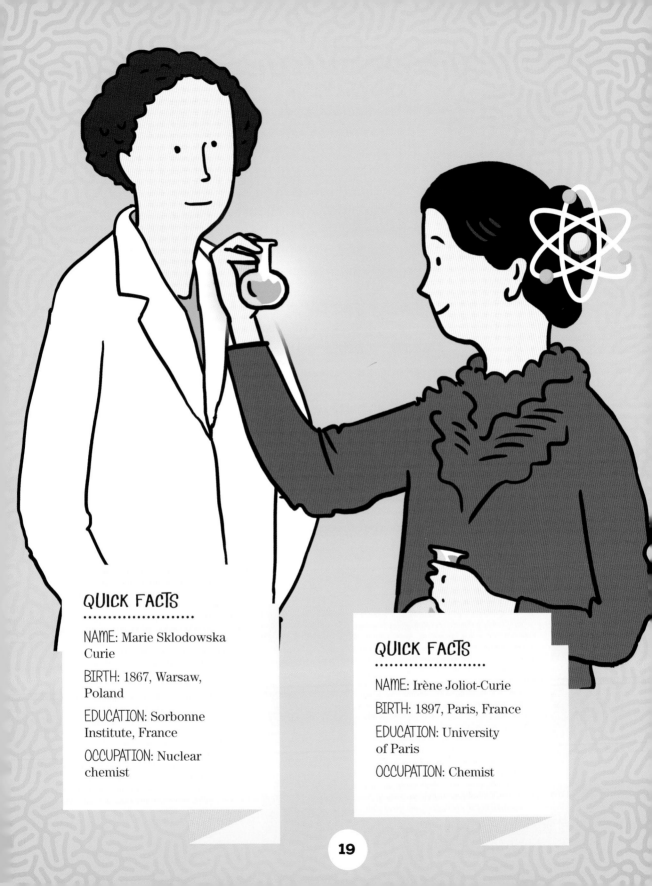

QUICK FACTS
....

NAME: Marie Sklodowska Curie

BIRTH: 1867, Warsaw, Poland

EDUCATION: Sorbonne Institute, France

OCCUPATION: Nuclear chemist

QUICK FACTS
....

NAME: Irène Joliot-Curie

BIRTH: 1897, Paris, France

EDUCATION: University of Paris

OCCUPATION: Chemist

> **❝ I believe that science has great beauty. ❞**
>
> Marie Curie

MARRIAGE TEAM

At the age of 24, Marie was admitted to the Sorbonne University in Paris, France. She was one of only a few women in a class of 2,000 men. Marie left her beloved family in Poland and moved to Paris. At the Sorbonne, she studied the physical sciences. She met fellow scientist Pierre Curie, and they married. Marie and Pierre began investigating a new area of chemistry: radioactivity.

GREAT DISCOVERIES

Inspired by the work of the French scientist Henri Becquerel, Marie and Pierre Curie tested a mineral called pitchblende. Becquerel had found the radioactive element uranium in the same mineral. The Curies isolated two new elements, radium and polonium, which were even more radioactive than uranium. In 1903, the Curies and Becquerel shared the Nobel Prize in Physics for the discovery.

In 1906, tragedy struck. Pierre was knocked down by a horse-drawn carriage and killed.

Marie spent her career studying the properties of radioactivity. Her work led to life-saving treatments.

Husband-and-wife team Pierre and Marie Curie work at their lab in Paris in the 1890s. Marie continued their work after Pierre's death in 1906.

Marie continued the research on radioactivity that she and Pierre had begun. She began cataloguing the properties of radioactive elements and their compounds. In 1911, Marie was awarded the Nobel Prize in Chemistry for producing radium as a pure metal.

ENDING AND BEGINNING

The dangers of radiation were not known at the time. Marie's exposure to radioactive substances eventually killed her. She contracted leukemia (a type of blood cancer) and died in 1934. Ironically, her work laid the foundations for certain cancer treatments.

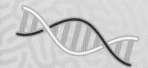

> ❝ **The farther the experiment is from theory, the closer it is to the Nobel Prize.** ❞
>
> Irène Joliot-Curie

IRENE JOLIOT-CURIE

The Curies' work lived on into the next generation. Their eldest daughter, Irène, was born in Paris on 12 September 1897. Irène developed an early interest in her parents' work. As a teenager during World War I (1914-1918), she helped her mother on a radiography team. They set up mobile units and X-rayed wounded men.

NEW STAR TEAM

Irène studied at the University of Paris and received her doctorate degree in chemistry in 1925. In 1926, she married a physicist, Frédéric Joliot, who had worked with her mother. The Joliot-Curies became another husband-and-wife team.

Irène (left) assisted her mother Marie in the laboratory from her teenage years onwards.

They studied and created new artificial radioactive elements. In 1935, they shared the Nobel Prize in Chemistry for this work. In 1938, their research into neutrons was a stepping stone in the development of nuclear fission.

Throughout Irène's career, she was keenly interested in the education of women. She was a member of many scientific societies and foreign academies. Irène died in Paris in 1956.

Frédéric and Irène Joliot-Curie at work in their laboratory.

NUCLEAR FAMILY

The Curies and Joliot-Curies are the family with most Nobel Prize winners. Marie won two prizes in physics and chemistry, the first person to be given the prize in two fields. Pierre shared the Nobel Prize in Physics, and Irène and Frédéric Joliot-Curie shared the Nobel Prize in Chemistry. Irène and Frédéric's children became scientists too. Their daughter, Hélène Langevin-Joliot, is a nuclear physicist, and their son, Pierre Joliot-Curie, is a biologist.

Marie Curie with children Eve (left) and Irène (right). Irène continued the Curie science dynasty.

Rachel Fuller Brown

American biochemist Rachel Fuller Brown developed one of the first fungus-fighting medicines, working with a colleague by post.

Rachel Fuller Brown was born in Springfield, Massachusetts, on 23 November 1898. Her father left the family in 1912, and her mother had to work to support the family. Rachel loved learning and worked hard at school. But it looked like she would not be able to afford to go to university. However, Henrietta F. Dexter, a wealthy friend of Rachel's grandmother, funded her tuition. She also received a small scholarship. She was able to go to Mount Holyoke College, in Massachusetts, to study history and chemistry.

QUICK FACTS

NAME: Rachel Fuller Brown

BIRTH: 1898, Springfield. Massachusetts, USA

EDUCATION: Mount Holyoke College, University of Chicago

OCCUPATION: Bacteriologist

> **" I hope for a future of equal opportunities and accomplishments for all scientists regardless of sex. "**

MASTERY BY DEGREES

Rachel earned her master's degree in organic chemistry from the University of Chicago. She wanted to continue studying but ran out of money. For the next three years, Rachel taught physics and chemistry at Francis Shimer school near Chicago. Eventually, she returned to the University of Chicago and received her doctorate degree in chemistry and bacteriology.

MOVING TO NEW YORK

in 1926, Rachel became assistant chemist at the New York State Division of Laboratories and Research in Albany, New York. Her initial work included finding faster and cheaper ways of screening people for syphilis. This is a disease that causes serious health issues if left untreated.

During World War II (1939–1945), antibiotics given to sick or wounded soldiers caused fungal infections. Rachel set her mind on finding a cure.

26

Rachel (left) and Elizabeth Lee Hazen pictured in the lab in the late 1950s, although they mostly worked by post.

Rachel also identified 40 different types of pneumonia (a bacterial or viral lung infection) and found blood serums (or antiserums) to tackle them.

In 1948, Rachel was chosen to work on an important project: finding a treatment for fungal infections. These infections were proving to be a problem for soldiers returning from World War II. Antibiotics had been used to treat many illnesses during wartime, but the side effects included fungal infections, for which there was no known cure.

POSTAL COLLABORATION

Microbiologist Elizabeth Lee Hazen, who worked in the department's New York City laboratory, was chosen to work with Rachel. The search was on for soil samples from around the world that might contain the right fungus-fighting bacteria.

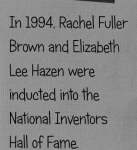

In 1994, Rachel Fuller Brown and Elizabeth Lee Hazen were inducted into the National Inventors Hall of Fame.

Rachel and Elizabeth communicated by post. Elizabeth would send Rachel bacteria from soil, posted in jars of soup. In her lab, Rachel would test the bacteria to see if they were effective in killing fungi. The first results were tested on small animals, but the animals died, so these drugs were not tested on humans.

In 1950, Rachel and Elizabeth discovered bacteria that would kill fungi but not harm the patient. The soil sample came from a friend's dairy farm in New York, very close to where Elizabeth lived. In 1954, the two women patented their antifungal drug and called it "Nystatin" in honour of the New York State laboratory where they had invented it. The patent for Nystatin was produced by E. R. Squibb drug company and went on to earn $13 million (£10.8 million).

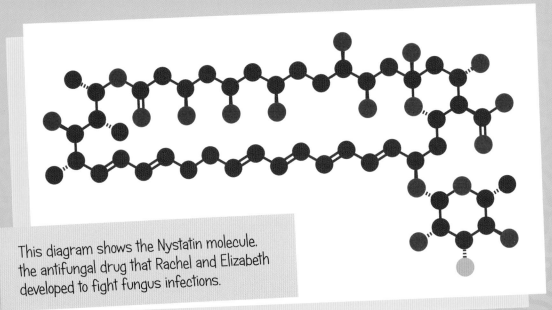

This diagram shows the Nystatin molecule, the antifungal drug that Rachel and Elizabeth developed to fight fungus infections.

GIVING BACK

Rachel Fuller Brown was very grateful for the financial support that had allowed her to study as a young women. She repaid her loan to Henrietta Dexter. Along with her successful career, it became Rachel's lifelong mission to encourage young women to study the sciences. She put all the profits made from Nystatin into a scheme to fund educational grants. Rachel died in 1980.

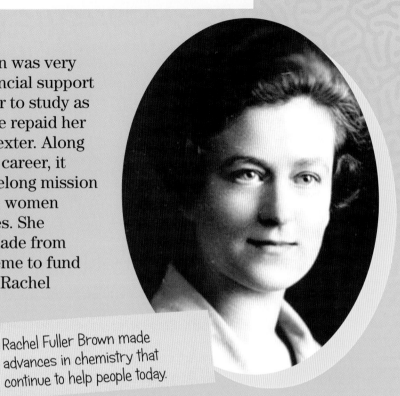

Rachel Fuller Brown made advances in chemistry that continue to help people today.

ELIZABETH LEE HAZEN

Microbiologist Elizabeth Lee Hazen was born in Rich, Mississippi, in 1885. She studied at Columbia University in New York, where she received a PhD. In 1931, Elizabeth began working at New York City's Division of Laboratories and Research, heading the Bacterial Diagnosis Laboratory. By the mid-1940s, she was working on a study to find bacteria that had fungus-fighting properties. This study led to her collaboration with Rachel, which resulted in the invention of Nystatin.

A photograph of Elizabeth Lee Hazen as a young woman in the early 1900s.

Dorothy Crowfoot Hodgkin

Egyptian-born British crystallographer who discovered the molecular structures of the drug penicillin and vitamin B12.

Dorothy Crowfoot Hodgkin was born in Cairo, Egypt, on 12 May 1910. Shortly afterwards, the family moved to Sudan. Her mother, Grace Mary Crowfoot, was a respected expert on textiles. Her father, John Crowfoot, worked in education. Later, both parents worked in archaeology in the Middle East. At about the age of 10, Dorothy became fascinated with minerals and crystals. A family friend gave her a chemistry set and helped her to analyse a mineral called ilmenite.

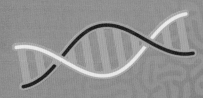

QUICK FACTS

NAME: Dorothy Crowfoot Hodgkin

BIRTH: 1910, Cairo, Egypt

EDUCATION: Oxford University, Cambridge University, England

OCCUPATION: Crystallographer

66 I was captured for life by chemistry and by crystals. 99

EARLY INTEREST

Dorothy and her sisters spent much of their childhood in Norfolk, England. At school, she and one of the other girls were allowed to join the boys in chemistry class. By the time she left school, she had decided to study science at college.

CUTTING EDGE RESEARCH

From 1928 to 1932, Dorothy studied at Somerville College, Oxford University. She received a degree in chemistry from Oxford University. With the help of her tutor, she decided to follow a newly developing field: X-ray crystallography. This type of X-ray imagery shows scientists the 3-D structure of complex organic molecules (groups of atoms). Dorothy soon found herself on the cutting edge of research.

In the 1930s, Dorothy carried out research using X-ray crystallography at both Oxford and Cambridge universities.

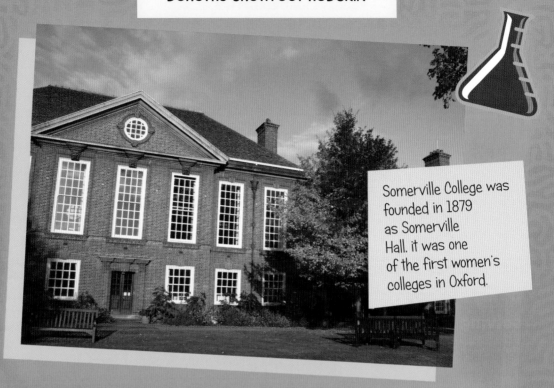

Somerville College was founded in 1879 as Somerville Hall. it was one of the first women's colleges in Oxford.

After graduating from Oxford, Dorothy moved to Cambridge University to do her PhD. She was supervised by John Desmond Bernal. He had worked with William Henry Bragg, who had developed the idea of using X-rays to "see" atoms and molecules in the 1910s. Together, Dorothy and Bernal worked on a number of important projects, and Dorothy's reputation as a highly skilled scientist grew. She became known as the "gentle genius".

FAMILY LIFE

Dorothy moved back to Somerville in 1934 to become a research fellow. She was a fellow and tutor in chemistry there from 1936 to 1977. In 1937, Dorothy married Thomas Hodgkin, an expert on African history. They started a family at Oxford.

Dorothy Crowfoot Hodgkin believed that scientific invention came with great responsibility. From 1976 to 1988, she was chairwoman of the Pugwash Movement. This international organization was set up by scientists to promote the peaceful use of scientific discoveries.

" I should not like to leave an impression that all structural problems can be settled by X-ray analysis. I seem to have spent much more of my life not solving ... them. **"**

Dorothy's parents helped with taking care of the grandchildren while Dorothy and Thomas worked. Dorothy studied the structure of cholesterol, a substance found in body tissues.

PENICILLIN AND B12

In the 1940s, Dorothy worked on the structure of the penicillin molecule. In 1949, she found that the molecule's parts were bound together in a very unusual way. This discovery led to new synthetic versions of penicillin, which were used for treating many illnesses.

Dorothy decoded the penicillin molecule. This photo of a model shows its molecular structure.

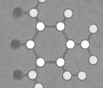

Dorothy Crowfoot Hodgkin working in her laboratory in 1964.

Dorothy took on another major project when she began investigating the structure of vitamin B12. Over six years, she took 2,500 X-ray photos of B12 crystals. Finally, with the help of a computer programmer from the University of California, Dorothy succeeded in cracking the code. She continued to work until late in her life, attending science and peace conferences around the world. She died in 1994.

AMAZING AWARDS

Throughout her lifetime, Dorothy won many awards for her scientific achievements. In 1964, she became only the third woman to receive the Nobel Prize in Chemistry. She received the Order of Merit in 1965, only the second woman to have been awarded it since nursing pioneer Florence Nightingale won it in 1907. In1976, Dorothy became the first and only woman to win the prestigious Copley Medal from the Royal Society in London.

ROSalind FranKlin

British chemist Rosalind Franklin is best known for her work in discovering the structure of DNA. She was also a pioneer in the field of X-ray diffraction.

On 25 July 25 1920, Rosalind Franklin was born into a wealthy Jewish family in London, United Kingdom. She showed early signs of talent for maths and science. When Rosalind was six years old, her aunt described her as being "alarmingly clever". Rosalind's parents sent her to Saint Paul's Girls' School. This was one of the few schools in London that prepared girls for a career. By the age of 15, Rosalind knew she wanted to be a scientist.

QUICK FACTS
....
NAME: Rosalind Elsie Franklin

BIRTH: 1920, London, UK

EDUCATION: Cambridge University

OCCUPATION: Physical chemist, crystallographer

66 Science and everyday life cannot and should not be separated. 99

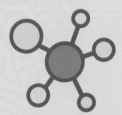

BACKGROUND STUDIES

In 1938, Rosalind entered Newnham College, Cambridge, UK. She graduated with a BA in 1941 and stayed at Cambridge for a year doing postgraduate research. In 1942, Rosalind joined the British Coal Utilisation Research Association to help with war work. Coal was a major fuel used in industry, and there were severe shortages during World War II. For four years, she researched the properties of coals and carbons on a microscopic level. Rosalind's work made it possible to classify types of coal and predict how they would act under different conditions.

THE STRUCTURE OF CRYSTALS

In 1947, Rosalind moved to Paris, France. With the help of a college friend, French scientist Adrienne Weill, she got a job working at Laboratoire Central des Services Chimique de l'Etat. Here she analysed carbon molecules using X-ray crystallography, or X-ray diffraction. This research helped in the development of new heat-resistant materials.

Rosalind taking a break from her busy work schedule. Her short life was mostly dedicated to research.

Rosalind's work led to an understanding of the structure of the DNA molecule.

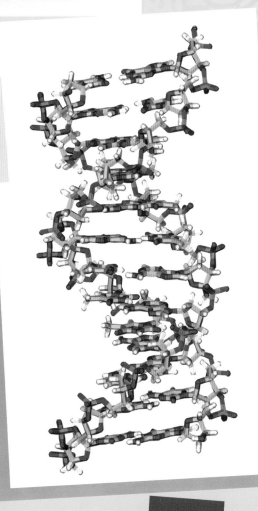

Rosalind became renowned among coal chemists. She also made many lasting friendships during her time in Paris.

BIG HELIX

Returning to England in 1951, Rosalind worked as a research associate in a laboratory at Kings College, London. She met Maurice Wilkins, assistant director of the lab. Rosalind was asked to investigate the structure of DNA, but Wilkins misunderstood her role and treated her as an assistant rather than an equal.

Rosalind and her assistant Raymond Gosling set to work taking X-ray diffraction images of DNA. She discovered that DNA had a wet and a dry form, and from the images, the wet form looked like a helix shape. Without Rosalind's knowledge, Wilkins showed one of her images to Francis Crick and James Watson, who were also researching DNA.

Outside the lab, Rosalind published many articles in scientific journals during her 16-year career. These included articles on the structure of coals and carbons, DNA and viruses.

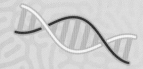

❝ My jaw fell open, and my pulse began to race. ❞

James Watson, on first seeing Photo 51

The image – known as Photo 51 – confirmed Watson and Crick's own, separate research. In 1953, they published their results in *Nature* magazine. They became famous for the discovery, but they never let Rosalind know that her image had formed part of their data.

PLANT VIRUSES

In 1953, Rosalind joined the crystallography lab at Birkbeck College, London. She studied the 3-D structure of viruses, especially the tobacco mosaic virus (TMV). This work helped scientists understand how to prevent and treat plant viruses, which was important to agriculture. It led to collaborations between Rosalind and other virus researchers in the UK and United States.

Rosalind looks through her microscope. She made important discoveries about plant viruses in the 1950s.

Rosalind's career was interrupted when she was diagnosed with ovarian cancer in autumn 1956. For the next 18 months, she underwent painful treatments but continued to work when she could.

Rosalind Franklin died on 16 April 1958, at only 37 years old. It was not until the 1970s that her role in the story of DNA was finally acknowledged.

James Watson (left) and Francis Crick pose with a model of DNA in 1953. They used Rosalind's data to confirm their findings.

PHOTO 51

Called "the most famous photograph in the world", Photo 51 gave key information for developing a model of DNA (the genetic code of living organisms). The X-ray crystallography photo was taken by Rosalind Franklin and her PhD student, Raymond Gosling, in May 1952. Without Rosalind's knowledge, her colleague Maurice Wilkins showed the photo to Francis Crick and James Watson. The "cross" pattern was the evidence that Crick and Watson needed to prove DNA was shaped like a helix.

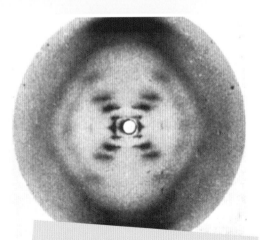

The cross pattern in Rosalind Franklin's Photo 51 shows that DNA is helix-shaped.

Timeline

1842	Ellen Swallow Richards is born on 3 December, in Dunstable, Massachusetts, United States.
1862	Agnes Pockels is born on 14 February, in Venice, Italy.
1862	Ellen Swallow Richards writes her home economics book, *The Chemistry of Cooking and Cleaning*.
1867	Marie Sklodowska Curie is born on 7 September, in Warsaw, Poland.
1876	Ellen Swallow Richards establishes the Women's Laboratory at MIT, where she works as an unpaid instructor.
1887	Ellen Swallow Richards becomes a water analyst for the New York State Board of Health.
1891	Agnes Pockels' research on surface science is published in *Nature* magazine.
1897	Irène Joliot-Curie is born on 12 September, in Paris, France.
1898	Rachel Fuller Brown is born on 23 November, in Springfield, Massachusetts, United States.
1903	Marie Curie wins the Nobel Prize in Physics with her husband Pierre for the discovery of radium and polonium.
1906	Pierre Curie is killed in a carriage accident.
1910	Dorothy Crowfoot Hodgkin is born on 12 May, in Cairo, Egypt.
1911	Marie Curie wins a second Nobel Prize for producing radium as a pure element.

1911	Ellen Swallow Richards dies.
1920	Rosalind Franklin is born on 25 July, London, UK.
1930s	Dorothy Crowfoot Hodgkin helps develop the field of X-ray crystallography.
1931	Agnes Pockels becomes the first women to win the Laura R. Leonard Prize.
1934	Marie Curie dies from leukemia, caused by working with radioactivity.
1935	Irène and Frédéric Joliot-Curie win the Nobel Prize in Chemistry for their discovery of artificial radioactivity.
1935	Agnes Pockels dies.
1940s	Dorothy Crowfoot Hodgkin decodes the penicillin and vitamin B12 molecules.
1950	Rachel Fuller Brown and Elizabeth Hazen discover bacteria that will kill fungal infections.
1952	After studying the structure of DNA with Raymond Gosling the previous year, Rosalind Franklin takes the famous Photo 51 showing the DNA helix shape.
1953	James Watson and Francis Crick announce their discovery of DNA structure, not mentioning Rosalind Franklin's role.
1954	Fuller and Hazen patent their Nystatin antifungal medicine.
1958	Rosalind Franklin dies at the age of 37 from ovarian cancer.
1962	Watson, Crick and Wilkins win the Nobel Prize in Chemistry for discovering the structure of DNA.
1994	Dorothy Crowfoot Hodgkin dies.

Gallery

The scientists covered in this book are only a few of the women who have advanced the study of chemistry, but here are more who achieved great things.

Gerty Theresa Cori (1896–1957)

A Czech-American biochemist who became the first American woman to win a Nobel Prize in science. Along with her husband, Carl Ferdinand Cori, Gerty discovered the way in which muscle cells use and store energy.

Marie Maynard Daly (1921–2003)

An American biochemist. In 1947, she became the first African American woman in the US to earn a PhD in chemistry. She carried out studies on cholesterol, sugars and proteins. She also set up a scholarship to help African American students.

Gertrude Belle Elion (1918–1999)

An American biochemist and pharmacologist. Her grandfather died from cancer when she was still in her teens, and she decided to become a scientist to fight diseases. In the 1940s, Gertrude began working for drug company Burroughs Wellcome. By 1950, she had developed leukemia-fighting substances called purines, which stopped cancerous white blood cells from duplicating in the body.

Stephanie Louise Kwolek (1923–2014)

An American chemist who worked at the DuPont Chemical company for 40 years. In 1965, she developed a group of strong synthetic fibres, including Kevlar, one of the most important synthetic fibres ever invented. Kevlar is used in aeroplanes, helmets and cables.

Marie-Anne Paulze Lavoisier (1758-1836)

A French chemist and noblewoman. She contributed to the work of her husband, French chemist Antoine Lavoisier, who revolutionized science by studying chemical reactions and naming many of the chemical elements.

Dame Kathleen Lonsdale (1903-1971)

An Irish crystallographer who moved to England as a child. In 1929, she studied the structure and properties of the mineral mellitene. Her results had a huge influence in the field of X-ray crystallography.

Mary Engle Pennington (1872-1952)

The first female laboratory chief of the US Food and Drug Administration (FDA) in 1905. Her research into bacteriology helped improve standards for handling dairy products and chicken. This made the food chain much safer.

SCIENCE NOW

Today, breakthroughs in chemistry happen every day. These include new ways to generate power and treat illnesses. Chemists develop cleaner fuel for cars, study how exposure to chemicals affects humans, and research how the brain works. They develop new treatments and drugs, and they tackle the effects of fracking and oil spills on the environment. More girls than ever before are studying for careers in STEM (Science, Technology, Engineering and Maths). Ask your teachers or careers adviser for more information.

Explore STEM clubs, workshops and summer schools for school-age students by searching online, or ask your teachers for help. If there isn't a club at your school, why not set up your own? And to find out how to get into science, visit STEM information sites, such as the WISE campaign at **www.wisecampaign.org.uk**

Glossary

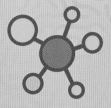

alchemy a type of science in the Middle Ages that tried to change common metals into gold

compound something that is made from a combination of elements

DNA substance that carries genetic information in the cells of living things

ecology science that deals with relationships between living things, such as people or plants, and their environment

element one of the basic substances made up of atoms of just one kind

fracking extracting oil and gas from underground rocks

matter substance that everything physical is made from

molecule the smallest amount of a substance that still has the properties of that substance. H_2O is a molecule of water.

patent document that gives a person or company the right to be the only producer of something, such as an invention or a drug, for a period of time

polonium radioactive element discovered by Marie and Pierre Curie

radioactive emitting a powerful and dangerous form of energy

radium radioactive element discovered by Marie and Pierre Curie

surface science study of what happens when two states, such as liquid and gas, come into contact with each other

syphilis serious sexually transmitted disease

virus tiny particle that causes a disease that can spread from one person to another, or from one animal to another

X-ray invisible ray that can pass through an object. Also, an image made using these rays that shows the inside of something, such as the human body, a plant or minerals.

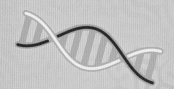

Further resources

Books

100 Women Who Made History, DK (Dorling Kindersley, 2017)

Trailblazers: 33 Women in Science Who Changed the World, Rachel Swaby (Random House Book for Young Readers, 2016)

What's Chemistry All About?, Alex Frith and Lisa Gillespie (Usborne Publishing, 2012)

Women in Science: 50 Fearless Pioneers Who Changed the World, Rachel Ignotofsky (Wren & Rook, 2017)

Websites

blog.sciencemuseum.org.uk/tag/chemistry
Visit the Science Museum's Chemistry blog page for lots of interesting articles about chemistry.

www.chemheritage.org/women-in-chemistry
Watch this amazing video about women in chemistry today, from the Chemical Heritage Foundation.

www.factmonster.com/spot/whmbios2.html
Visit Fact Monster's informative site, and learn about the women who made a difference in science.

www.rsc.org/diversity/175-faces
Read biographies of famous female and male chemists, both living and historical, on the Royal Society of Chemistry website.

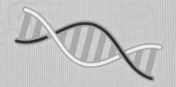

index